ANANTNAAG

SHOBHIT AGARWAL

Made with ♥ on the Notion Press Platform
www.notionpress.com

Contents

Preface *v*

1. Chapter 1: A Prince In Disguise 1
2. Chapter 2: Shadows Strengthen 6
3. Chapter 3: When Science Meets Sorcery 11
4. Chapter 4: Nature's Wrath 21
5. Chapter 5: A New Dawn 27

Preface

Prince Anantnaag rules the secret kingdom of Naaglok hidden deep in the jungles. With powers over nature and illusion, the naagloks live in hidden peace. But this changes when ruthless scientist Dr. Ashok arrives, seeking to exploit the naagloks' gifts for his experiments.

Through his spies in the human world, Anantnaag learns of Ashok's plans. But breaking the naagloks' most sacred law to not interact with humans, Anantnaag takes a risky mission. Disguised as a man, he befriends Meera, a kind teacher unaware of the supernatural. Hoping her kindness can sway others, Anantnaag struggles with his feelings and duty.

Meanwhile, Ashok's forces skirmish with the naagloks, causing casualties. Some in Naaglok feel Anantnaag is unfit to rule, seeing humans as the enemy. They form a rebellion with Ashok, seeking to overthrow Anantnaag and give the scientists what they want.

When Meera gets caught in the crossfire, Anantnaag must unleash his full powers to save her and defend his people. But Ashok's mysterious benefactor proves a formidable foe. Through tangled lies and stunning magical battles, can Anantnaag preserve the peace and win Meera's heart? Or will the naagloks at last face destruction by Science's hand?

ONE

Chapter 1: A Prince in Disguise

Prince Anantnaag Feels the Burden of Leadership
Prince Anantnaag stood on the balcony of his royal apartments, gazing out over the mystical kingdom of Naaglok. As the soft dawn light filtered through the lush rainforest, he took in the familiar sights and sounds that always soothed his soul.

But this morn, an unease lurked in the air. Anantnaag's sharp senses detected whispers of fear from his people drifting up from the villages below. They huddled in their homes, peering nervously out for any sign of the intruders threatening their peaceful haven.

Anantnaag's spies had brought grim news - the ruthless human scientist Dr. Ashok was encroaching into their territory, intent on exploiting the naagloks' magical gifts. Though Naaglok's cloaking illusions kept it well hidden, the latest attacks proved the barriers were weakening against this formidable foe.

The weight of responsibility for his people's safety pressed down on Anantnaag's young shoulders. As prince by birth and guardian by choice, it was his duty to protect Naaglok. But how could he vanquish a menace that did not play by their rules of honor? Violence would only invite more troubles, yet allowing the poacher to plunder risked the kingdom's doom.

A flicker of movement below caught Anantnaag's keen sight. His old adviser Vishnu was leading a growing faction of naagloks who questioned Anantnaag's leadership. Could even his own people turn against him if he failed?

Doubt clouded Anantnaag's mind like an incoming storm. He knew challenging times were upon Naaglok. The prince could only pray to the gods of nature for wisdom, and hope his people stayed united in the face of the threat luring at their borders. For if Naaglok fell, all of their kind would surely follow into darkness. As Prince Anantnaag consulted with his most trusted adviser, Nagini, about the troubling news from his spies.

"Dr. Ashok's forces grow bolder by the day," Anantnaag told her gravely. "If we do not act soon, I fear even our strongest illusions will not hide Naaglok from his pursuit of power and secrets."

Nagini nodded solemnly. "The elders will never condone direct involvement with humans. But staying idle risks far greater harm. You must seek allies beyond our borders, Anantnaag my prince, as is your duty to our kingdom."

Anantnaag knew the weighty step he must take. "Then I will take human form myself to befriend those who can aid our cause. My spies observed a kindhearted teacher, Meera, who shows Naaglok's ways to the village children. Perhaps through her gentle nature, others' hearts may be opened too."

Though betraying sacrosanct laws, saving his realm demanded sacrifices. Anantnaag placed his faith in the goodwill still left in the human world. But would Naaglok understand the risk he must take for their protection? And if he succeeded, what challenges would this new path hold for the prince of the serpents? Only time would reveal the answers, as Anantnaag began his covert mission to contact the outsiders called humans. , Anantnaag took on a human guise and ventured into the bustling town bordering Naaglok's forests. Though unfamiliar with their ways, his keen eyes took in all the sights, sounds and scents of this foreign world.

Weaving between crowds, a sweet song drifted to his ears - the laughter of children at play. Following the melody, Anantnaag came upon a small schoolhouse. Through its open doors and windows, he glimpsed Meera teaching her pupils with a smile.

"Now, who can name these rainforest flowers and what special powers they possess?" she asked. Eager hands shot up, and Meera called on a shy girl. Though her answer was wrong, Meera praised her effort instead of scolding. Another boy had the right response, and she encouraged the class to applaud his knowledge.

Anantnaag was struck by Meera's patience and gifts for bringing out the best in her students. Though humans, the spark in their eyes showed their souls remained uncorrupted. Perhaps, with caring teachers like Meera, the children's generation could view Naaglok's people not as threats but friends.

As the lesson ended and the kids raced off to play, Anantnaag saw his chance. With a Deep Bow and request to learn more about rainforest lore, he first approached the kind teacher Meera, hoping her gentle spirit may prove a key ally for his kingdom in these dark times., Anantnaag intercepted Meera at the school gates as she was leaving for the day.

"Miss Meera, may I compliment you on your way with children?" he said with a kindly smile. "You bring out the light in them."

Meera looked surprised by the praise from this stranger. "Why, thank you sir. It does my heart good to see them learn and play."

Anantnaag nodded. "You are a rare soul. These villagers are lucky to have a teacher who cares so deeply."

Meera blushed at the unexpected flattery. "You speak with more thought than most men here. Might I ask your name, sir?"

"I am Anantnaag. And there is more I wish to learn from you, if you'll accept my company on your walk home." He bowed respectfully. "Your students flock to you for your patience. Perhaps we older ones also have much yet to learn."

Intrigued by Anantnaag's thoughtful demeanor, unlike the brusque local men, Meera found herself agreeing. And so began their stroll together, the prince of serpents drawing the kind teacher into conversation, hoping her gentle spirit may yet prove an ally for his kingdom in the trials to come. That evening, seeds of dissent were being sown in the depths of Naaglok's emerald forests. In a glade lit by sacred lamps, Vishnu met his growing circle of rebels.

The crown prince cavorts with humans while we suffer attacks! Vishnu spat. Anantnaag is too weak to defend our homeland.

Murmurs of agreement rose from the gathering. We've prospered for eons obeying the old laws, said one elder naaglok. Yet now when we most need a fighter, our prince betrays tradition.

Vishnu feigned sorrow as he stoked their frustration. If only we had leadership willing to harness what power we can find, even from outsiders. Then poachers like the scientist would tremble before us!

The rebels pondered this talk of using human knowledge rather than shunning it. Might embracing change ensure our dominion over all nature, as the gods intended? Anantnaag only preaches patience and diplomacy, blind to the true dangers.

Very well, Vishnu declared with an oily smile. When the time is right, we shall unite with this Dr. Ashok and his kind, seizing control of Naaglok's destiny. And any who stand in our righteous path will be swept aside... On the bustling lanes of the market square next day, Anantnaag happened upon Meera doing her daily shopping. Might I aid you with those heavy bags, my friend? he offered politely.

Meera was surprised yet again by the thoughtful prince's appearance. You need not trouble yourself, sir, she smiled. But Anantnaag insisted on carrying her parcels, falling into step beside her.

As they wandered amongst the stalls, Anantnaag listened closely to Meera's words, hoping to better understand humans through her kindness. Your students are lucky indeed, he remarked. Though some see only chaos, with your eyes I glimpse hope still remains here.

Meera studied her new acquaintance, puzzled yet intrigued by his insightful ways so unlike others. You speak in riddles sometimes, sir! she laughed. But your company is refreshing for this tired teacher.

Reaching her door, Anantnaag bade Meera farewell with thanks. But know that should you ever need an ear, this stranger would gladly listen, he added with a bow. Perhaps through our talks, each could find new purpose in these uncertain days. And so their bond strengthened further, as Anantnaag's covert mission to aid Naaglok through this unlikely ally began to unfold. As their talks continued, Meera and Anantnaag found common ground in their love for the natural world. Your students see the beauty in each flower that my people know by heart, Anantnaag remarked.

Meera sighed. But this world values so-called progress over stewardship. The adults round here scoff if you question cutting forests for farms.

Anantnaag nodded grimly. Some pursuits of power endanger the balance all depends on. But without the roots of reverence you plant, how soon till darker forces take hold?

A kinship was blossoming between these unlikely allies, each noticing in the other a thoughtfulness lacking in their own. Yet Anantnaag also felt stirrings of another emotion he dared not name. As prince of Naaglok, attachments beyond his realm were forbidden.

And so he struggled between duty and his heart's longing. Meera's kindness rekindled hopes fading from his people, proving perhaps humans need not always be enemies. But to reveal his true nature risked shattering the trust now growing between them, endangering all he strived to protect. Anantnaag could only pray his deceptions would not be the undoing of both their peoples. That night as the moon rose, ominous portents reached Anantnaag's keen ears. From deep within the slumbering jungle, cries and clashes echoed — the unmistakable sounds of skirmish.

Alarmed, Anantnaag summoned his scout Nagini. "Fly to the borderlands and return with news," he commanded.

Within moments, her small form flitted into the shadows.

Weighing heavily, long hours passed before Nagini reappeared. "Dr. Ashok's men grow bolder, my prince," she hissed gravely. "Casualties were inflicted this eve on both sides."

Rage and fear stirred within Anantnaag's heart. How long before this threat engulfed all of Naaglok? Too much was at stake now to waver.

Resolved, Anantnaag spoke. "Double patrols within our realm. No trespasser shall pass unchecked." To Nagini he said, "Inform our spies - we must learn this enemy's intentions, strengths and weaknesses."

As Anantnaag gazed into the deep forest, a flicker of movement caught his eye — was it figment or foe lurking there? He was more determined than ever to protect his people, whatever it took. Naaglok's fate hung by a thread, and it was up to their prince to sever it or be destroyed.

TWO

Chapter 2: Shadows Strengthen

The jungle shadows grew longer as Dr. Ashok's men pushed deeper into the dense foliage. They had engaged a patrol of Naagloks earlier, inflicting casualties before withdrawing. Among the fallen was the elderly king who had chosen to stay behind and cover his people's escape, buying them precious time with his life.

Anantnaag paced the palace balconies, eyes scanning the treeline for any sign of the returning patrol. Nagini joined him, bearing grave news. "The patrol was ambushed far from our borders. The humans fought without care for life." Anantnaag frowned at this escalation. "And what of our king?" Nagini lowered her head. "He fought valiantly but has entered the forest eternal. One more was lost - a young scout named Kaa."

Anantnaag closed his eyes against the loss. Kaa had only recently come of age, his skills barely blossomed. That he should fall to the whims of ruthless men galled Anantnaag deeply. When he opened his eyes again, they had hardened with resolve. "Double the border patrols. I want every movement in the trees reported. It is time we learned more of this Dr. Ashok and why he disrupts the peace of the jungle." Nagini nodded, swiftly departing to carry out his orders. Anantnaag knew darker days lied ahead, and he would do all in his power to steer his people through the storm. Meera glanced up from her lesson plans as Anantnaag entered the classroom. His thoughts seemed far away. "Is all well?" she asked gently.

Anantnaag started. "Forgive me, I did not mean to disturb." He sank onto a desk, fingers pleating a loose thread. "My people face troubles and it weighs on my mind."

Meera laid a hand on his arm. "What troubles you carry alone, you carry double. Please, let me ease your burden if I can."

Anantnaag looked into her kind eyes and found solace there. "I am prince to my people. It is my duty to protect them, but some threat moves in the jungle I do not yet understand. Men skulk where they ought not. My patrols have faced them and today I lost subjects dear."

He told her only part of the truth, omitting Naaglok's secret. But the truth of a leader's burden and doubts he shared, hoping for her counsel. Meera listened patiently. "Dark times often precede the dawn. Have faith the answers will come. For now, focus on keeping hope alive in your people's hearts as you do in yours."

Her wisdom comforted Anantnaag. "You are a gift, Meera. Thank you for hearing me and lifting my spirit when it is low." Vishnu paced before the assembled rebels. The old king is dead, a child stolen from our homes! Dr. Ashok's men grow bolder while our prince spends his days cavorting with humans.

The rebels muttered angrily. This is a sign, Vishnu continued. The humans can never be trusted. Anantnaag is blinded by his care for outsiders. We must seize control before it is too late!

From the crowd emerged Nagini. Do not let fear rule your hearts. The prince but seeks understanding of our foe. Violence should always be a final act, not the first.

Vishnu sneered. Always so cautious, Nagini. While you whisper of patience, our borders bleed. The humans must be driven out before they learn our secrets. Only then will Naaglok be safe.

The rebels rumbled in approval but Nagini held up a hand. Be careful of spreading rumors, Vishnu. Our people sense unease and look to us for guidance. Wisdom, not action in haste, is needed now more than ever. The meeting ended in uneasy truce as the factions went their separate ways, minds clouded by doubt., Under the shade of a mighty banyan, Anantnaag spun tales of the deep jungle for Meera's delight. With illusion magic he gave life to chital fleeing through brush, elephants bathing at the riverbend. Meera laughed in wonder, fear banished from this secret bower.

Anantnaag smiled seeing her joy, his troubles swept aside. Yet as a peacock burst shining from his hands, Meera looked not to the glamour but to its maker. His eyes held eons she could not fathom; power swirled just below the surface of his skin. Anantnaag appeared no different from any man, and yet...

He sensed her uncertainty and let the illusion melt. Meera, I— Her words tumbled out. "What magic is this? You are no ordinary person." Anantnaag feared driving her away but saw only curiosity, not fright, in her face.

"A secret I must keep, as my people depend on it. Know only that I mean you no harm." Meera regarded him. Her heart said trust this man, but her mind reeled with questions unanswered. For now, she chose to believe. "Then your secrets are safe with me, as I hope mine with you in time." Anantnaag smiled, comforted., Deep in his secret laboratory, Dr. Ashok probed the captive naaglok for signs of its mystical gifts. But the creature lay weak and unresponsive despite all efforts.

A shadow fell across the cell. Ashok turned to find his benefactor observing coldly. Your progress disappoints, the figure remarked. I spared no expense so you might unlock nature's secrets. Instead you coddle this thing.

Dr. Ashok bristled. Torture will yield nothing, only death. I am a scientist, not a butch—

The benefactor's voice lashed like a whip. Results, Ashok, or our arrangement ends. I care not how you achieve them, only that you succeed.

As the presence swept away, Ashok snarled and took a scalpel to the naaglok's skin. Powers beyond science were at work here, and he would tear them free whether the creature willed it or not. Darker days yet lay ahead in the jungle, as two driven minds pushed further into the shadows of their obsessions.,, Consequences be damned. Vishnu stalked through the laboratory, lip curled in distaste. Ashok circled him predatorily. State your purpose, snake, before I feed you to my pets.

Vishnu hissed. We share a common foe in Prince Anantnaag. I can guide your men to Naaglok's hidden city, if you pledge alliance to my cause when it is mine.

Ashok clasped hands behind his back. And why should I trust one of those abominations? Your kind has eluded science for long enough. Better I flay your secrets from your skin.

Patient as stone, Vishnu met his predatory gaze. Torture will avail you nothing. Only I know the paths through the deep jungle, the illusions that shield their home. Aid me and all its mysteries will be unlocked for your experiments. Defy me and you will wander those woods until death claims your rotting corpse.

Ashok bared his teeth in a grin. You drive a hard bargain, snake. But I have faced tougher deals. You will lead my men to this Naaglok. And when its treasures are mine to claim...we shall see who proves the tougher creature. Agree to these terms?" Meera gently dried a small bird's damp feathers by the creekside. Its wing hung at an awkward angle where it had fallen from the nest. But under Meera's care, its cheeps grew stronger each day.

Anantnaag watched, transfixed, as she nursed the little thing with drops of water and bits of berry. Your compassion knows no bounds, he said softly. This one is lucky to have found you.

Meera smiled, hope shining in her eyes. All beings deserve care in times of trouble, would you not say? Her wisdom warmed him. His guard had fallen without him realizing, drawn in by her light.

Seeing her nurture new life inspired him. My people face threats, as this one did in the fall from its nest. I strive to guide them through this storm as you have this bird. But the way forward remains unclear...

He told her then of Naaglok - its magic, his duty, Ashok's encroachment. A great weight lifted as her acceptance wrapped around him. You are noble to shoulder such responsibility, Anantnaag. Have faith in yourself, and in them, as I do in this little one's strength to fly again. Her belief rekindled his own., The jungle tones rang out in alarm - intruders approached. Anantnaag felt Meera's danger and left with urgency. Through shadows he raced, coming upon the skirmish's edge where Dr. Ashok's men hacked at undergrowth.

Vines snapped from the earth, ensnaring them as Anantnaag commanded the trees. But the men's black weapons spat fire, felling ancients in return. Anantnaag summoned a mist to shroud their movements even as arrow and bullet grazed his arm. How far they've pushed within our borders, he seethed.

A warning cry pierced the clash - Meera had wandered into the battlefield's heart trying to stem the violence. Seeing her, the ruffians closed in with wicked intent. Anger flared in Anantnaag hotter than the sun. The earth rumbled and split; a great serpent rose at his call and bore down upon the men with thunderous wrath.

The battle ceased. Anantnaag went to Meera, embracing her unharmed form. His magic and concern unveiled, all that was hidden now lay bare between them under the jungle's watchful eyes. Her touch whispered understanding; his whispered a plea never to leave his side again. Anantnaag's serpent tossed the last man from its coils. The battlefield fell silent as his magic retreated into the earth. Though bloodied, no lives were lost on either side - Anantnaag had shown restraint.

But as the dazed men fled, a presence lingered, observing. It approached Anantnaag unseen. You fight well for a mystic, the Entity spoke in his mind. But your home intrigues me, as does your power. Know that I've set my sights on Naaglok now.

Anantnaag whirled, senses straining for the intruder but finding only shadows. Reveal yourself! he commanded.

What business have you with my people?

Laughter echoed through the trees. All will be revealed in time, prince. For now, savor what victories you can. The shadows stirred, and the Entity vanished as swiftly as it had come.

THREE

Chapter 3: When Science Meets Sorcery

Vishnu's faction of dissenting naagloks had grown emboldened in their opposition to Anantnaag's leadership. When the prince ordered increased patrols of the borderlands after the recent skirmish, Vishnu openly defied the command.

"We will not endanger more of our own on wild goose chases into those dangerous woods," Vishnu declared before the assembled naagloks. Murmurs of approval rippled through the crowd that had gathered.

Nagini stepped forward, her scales glimmering in the dappled sunlight that filtered through the dense jungle canopy. "Prince Anantnaag commands out of duty to protect all of Naaglok," she said calmly yet firmly. "These are difficult times that require unity, not division."

"Unity behind a leader whose policies invite destruction!" Vishnu retorted. "While he cavorts with humans, Dr. Ashok's men advance further into our domain. We must meet force with force, not hope these invaders lose interest and leave of their own accord."

The rebel naagloks roared in support of Vishnu's statement. Nagini shook her head sadly, knowing reason fell on deaf ears among those drunk on ambition and eager for confrontation. Anantnaag watched from a distance, his heightened senses picking up every word. The challenges to his leadership mounted along with the grave threats his people faced. Troubled times lay ahead for the kingdom of Naaglok. Slipping unseen into the dense jungle, Anantnaag made his way to a familiar glade where he often met Meera. As expected, she was there among the flowering shrubs, fingers trailing gently over vivid petals dyed crimson by the setting sun's light.

"Meera," Anantnaag said softly as not to startle her. She turned with a smile that faded at his troubled expression. "What troubles you so, my friend?"

Anantnaag relayed Vishnu's defiance and the growing unrest, as well as his concerns over Dr. Ashok's intentions. "My people are in danger and there are those who would see me fail," he sighed. "The burdens of leadership have never felt so heavy."

Meera reached out and clasped his hands in hers. "You care so deeply, as any good leader should. Do not lose hope - there are also those who believe in you." Her warm embrace surrounded him, and for a moment Anantnaag took comfort in pushing aside his cares and simply feeling the compassion of a true friend. Her faith strengthened his resolve to meet the challenges ahead. Anantnaag and Meera's moment of solace was shattered by crashing sounds of conflict in the forest. They broke apart, senses alert as an unnatural quiet fell heavy among the trees.

Without a word, Anantnaag sped silently through the dense undergrowth with Meera keeping pace behind him. Soon they caught sight of the source of disturbance - a group of naagloks was being ambushed by men wielding nets and strange weapons that spit fire and noise.

One of the naagloks cried out as a net enveloped her, her magical aura flickering uselessly against the entangling ropes. Anantnaag growled and flung out his hands, summoning vines that wrapped tight around the captors. But more men emerged from the shadows, driving the outnumbered naagloks back with shouts and flashing tools.

Meera stifled a gasp as one of the naagloks was struck down before Anantnaag's anguished eyes. Rage and power swelled within him - these invaders had crossed a line in assaulting his kin on their own soil. His incantation shook the forest as ancient magics answered his call. The battle had truly begun. Anantnaag unleashed the full breadth of his power, magic erupting forth in a kaleidoscope of unearthly beauty and wrath. The very forest seemed to come alive at his command, trees twisting in an exotic dance as roots ensnared the invaders.

Meera watched in awe and not a little fear - this was no longer the gentle man she knew, but a creature of legend. Anantnaag shed his mortal guise, serpentine form spiraling upwards as jeweled scales rippled into view. Hands melted into claws that grasped at shadows while his once-kind eyes blazed with otherworldly light.

All around, the forest answered his call. Vines coiled tight as the felled naaglok was borne swiftly away to safety. Illusions shimmered - men suddenly found themselves facing their worst nightmares while unseen assailants harried them from every direction.

Anantnaag's voice echoed with the might of a raging storm as he challenged the ambushers in a language as old as the earth. Meera beheld the majesty of his true nature and power, even as a part of her quailed at such raw forces unleashed. Her view of the world would never be the same again. The battle came to a sudden end as Dr. Ashok's men broke and fled into the night, bound by invisible shackles. Anantnaag recalled his magics, form shrinking back into a human semblance.

He turned to Meera, dread in his eyes at what she might think of him now. But she stepped forward without hesitation. Are you well? she asked, scanning for injuries. I must understand, she pleaded. Help me see as you see.

Anantnaag nodded slowly, weariness seeping into his bones. The costs of the clash weighed on him - none of his kin lay dying thanks to their skills in illusion and sorcery, but no war was without cost. Dr. Ashok's men would not relent so easily in their attacks.

Meera wanted nothing more than to comfort her friend, yet her mind reeled with the revelations of this day. All she had known was upturned. Though her heart affirmed her care for Anantnaag remained unchanged, her rattled thoughts needed time. A gulf had opened between their worlds that would not easily close again. Both knew darker days were yet to come. Vishnu watched the skirmish from afar, eyes gleaming. With Anantnaag's display of power, none could deny the true threat Naaglok faced. That night, he gathered his followers once more.

See how even Meera, who professed friendship, recoiled from our prince's true nature, Vishnu hissed. Humans will never accept what they do not understand. Anantnaag's trust has left our borders vulnerable, our kin attacked on their own soil.

Unease rippled through the assembled naagloks as he stroked their fears. Anantnaag endangers all with his games among humans. Only through our ways can Naaglok's sovereignty be secured. Follow me, and together we shall force these invaders out - by persuasion, if Anantnaag will not lead, or by force if we must.

Vishnu's poison continued spreading, doubt and discord clouding clear judgment. In the aftermath of battle, Anantnaag faced his gravest crisis yet - a rising rebellion that threatened to tear Naaglok apart from within its own borders. Dark designs were unfolding in the kingdom's heart. Anantnaag sought solace in the sacred grove where a towering icon of Lord Shiva kept eternal vigil. He knelt before the divine statue, sorrowful yet resolved.

"O great Mahadev, grant me your renowned poise and strength to end this discord." Anantnaag prayed. Shafts of moonlight seemed to embrace him in response, infusing renewed purpose.

He emerged from the grove transformed, a serene yet immutable force of righteousness. Steeling himself, Anantnaag confronted Vishnu's insurgents. But the sly serpent had slithered away under cover of dark, sowing yet more seeds of chaos.

Distraught rebels cried of Vishnu's capture, fueling panic that Anantnaag's enemies held sway. In truth, Vishnu's aim was to divide Naaglok from within while escaping fair judgment.

The turmoil swelled, Anantnaag's rule hanging by a thread as he struggled to quell hysteria and reveal the serpent's deceptions. Darker magics were afoot, and Lord Shiva's boon alone might not suffice to save Naaglok from the looming tempest. Meera's confusion and uncertainty led her to avoid the forest paths where she knew Anantnaag might appear. Her mind replayed their encounter, flickering between wonder and unease.

Returning to her village immersed in thought, she sensed something amiss. People scattered too swiftly at her approach, furtive whispers dogging her steps. What strangeness was this?

In the schoolhouse, all seemed unchanged yet not. Lessons lay abandoned, idle chalk gathering dust as if some essential spark had fled both adult and child alike. Meera's questions went unmet with averted eyes.

A shadow hung over the village, some outside will claiming dominion where once song and laughter ruled unchecked. Meera stood alone questioning all she knew, Naaglok's plight and her own heart's test coming into ever sharper conflict under the gathering gloom. Forces beyond her experience were closing in from all sides, and even this safe haven could no longer shelter her doubts., Meera tossed and turned, tormented by vivid dreams. She witnessed Naaglok's fair jungle cloaked in an unnatural fog, trees rotting where once life teemed. Dr. Ashok strode amid the ruins, naagloks frozen in horror below his lurid laboratory walls.

Then the scene changed. Her village stood deserted under a red sky, an anguished howl echoing bereft of solace. From the veil of clouds emerged a colossal shadow, face unseen yet malign will tangible. It regarded her tiny form with infinite malice before grinding its claws together in cruel anticipation.

Meera awoke screaming, horror lingering at the edges of her mind's eye. What darkness had intruded to so afflict her rest? She sensed no ordinary nightmare, but a dramatic portent - if Naaglok fell, what evil might next set its sight on her gentle corner of the world?

Dawn brought her no surcease, insights haunting her waking hours. Anantnaag faced threats beyond any mortal foe, and in his struggle was embroiled the fate of realms unseen. She could remain on the sidelines no longer - Naaglok's plight was now her own., There are no more specified beats provided for Chapter 3. Based on the story outline and progression so far, here is a possible conclusion to the chapter:

Meera resolved to venture back into the forest and seek Anantnaag, determined to offer her support however she could. As she made her way through the dense foliage, an eerie silence hung in the air.

A rustling sound made her turn, coming face to face with Vishnu in his serpent form. "The prince has fallen," he hissed menacingly. "Naaglok is mine to command now."

Before Meera could react, Vishnu struck with lightning speed, injecting her with a foul poison. As her vision darkened, she heard mocking laughter and sensed a looming threat closing in on the defenseless kingdom.

When Meera awoke, she found herself in a dim cave, Anantnaag's prone form beside her. With a gasp, she saw his aura flickering weakly. Had Vishnu's treachery spelled doom for the rightful ruler of Naaglok? Panic and resolve swelled in Meera's heart - she must find a way to save Anantnaag and help him reclaim his kingdom before it was too late.

Thus ends another chapter in the unfolding saga, with the villain's schemes advancing as peril mounts for both Anantnaag and his beloved Naaglok. Darkness looms on the horizon as the stage is set for new battles to come in the next part of the tale. Here is the beginning of Chapter 4 continuing the storyline:

Vishnu's influence had caused chaos in Naaglok. Anantnaag called an urgent meeting of the tribal elders in the crater caves beneath the Misty Peaks.

"My brothers, these are troubled times," said Anantnaag. "Vishnu has turned many against our cause through his silver tongue and dark deeds. But we cannot lose hope - it is all some have left."

Nagini spoke up. "Vishnu refuses to see reason. His men grow bolder near the borders despite your orders. They hunger for revenge against the invaders but may cause more harm than good."

One of the elders, Kaa, agreed. "Vishnu seeks nothing but power. I have heard rumblings of a plot against the crown."

Anantnaag sighed heavily. "Then the insurgency runs deeper than I feared. Vishnu must be stopped before he destroys us from within. But we cannot reign destruction upon our own. I seek an alternative."

Just then, a scout named Roshi rushed in. "My prince! Dr. Ashok's men have been sighted near the Eastern Glades. It seems they mean to incite further conflict."

Anantnaag rose, determination in his eyes. "Then I must intervene before blood is shed on either side. Gather your forces - we will show Vishnu's followers a better way through courage and wisdom, not conflict."

With that, he slithered off into the night, hoping it was not too late to prevent a civil war from tearing Naaglok asunder. Nagini hissed in frustration as Anantnaag gathered his forces. My prince, you hesitate when urgency is needed, she urged. Vishnu stops at nothing in his quest for power.

Anantnaag sighed. Violence will only beget more violence, Nagini. Our way is one of patience and understanding. Though Vishnu has lost his way, force is not the answer.

But what if peaceful solutions fail? Time is a luxury we may not have. You are beloved by your people - they follow your strength, not weakness. Show Vishnu you will not stand by as Naaglok tears itself apart. Assert your rightful rule before -

Her words were cut short by Roshi's return. My prince - the Eastern Glades are engulfed in battle! Vishnu's men and the humans fight, heaving curses and bloodshed. You must intervene before the edge is lost...and all is destroyed.

Anantnaag exchanged a grave look with Nagini. It seems peaceful solutions will have to wait. Rally the guard - we fly at once to save what remains of the glade, and any caught in the crossfire. This day, courage may be the only choice to prevent further calamity. And so help me, Vishnu will be brought to justice for the chaos he has wrought.

With a mighty leap, Anantnaag took wing, hoping he was not already too late. Meera's dreams had been troubled since witnessing Anantnaag's true nature. Trying to understand, she walked the forest path, hoping to find him.

Doubts clouded her mind. Was Anantnaag really the gentle soul she knew? Or had Vishnu's words poisoned her view? Only by speaking with Anantnaag could she hope to find the truth.

As she walked, memories surfaced - Anantnaag's passion for the jungle's beauty, his calm assurances in troubled times. Could one so attuned to nature harbor darkness in his heart? Meera didn't think so.

Breaking into a run, she followed the babble of a distant stream, believing Anantnaag often found solace there.

Emerging into a glade, she stopped suddenly. Before her, the Eastern Glades blazed with unnatural flames, figures twisted in combat among the trees.

With a sinking heart, Meera realized the danger Anantnaag and his people faced. In that moment, her feelings crystallized - she cared not for his form, only his true self: noble, protective, and intensely beloved. Clenching her fists, Meera knew she would stand by Anantnaag's side, come what may. Steeling herself, Meera plunged into the burning glade. As she darted between the snarling combatants, a sinister laugh rang out. Following the sound, she arrived at a shadowed glen to see Vishnu meeting with Dr. Ashok.

"With Anantnaag out of the way, Naaglok will fall," Vishnu hissed. "Your scientists will have free rein over my people."

Dr. Ashok smiled coldly. "And you'll have the power you crave, handing over their secrets. Once I harness that magic, none will stand in science's way!"

Meera gasped in horror. Their true motive was tyranny, not defense. At the sound, Vishnu spun, eyes flashing murderously as he caught sight of her.

"You!" he snarled, lunging with fangs bared. Meera scrambled away, dodging between the trees as Vishnu gave chase. She had to warn Anantnaag - their enemies were more sinister than imagined, aiming to enslave not defend. Praying she could reach him in time, Meera fled into the burning depths of the jungle, the crackle of flames and Vishnu's rageful shrieks ringing behind her. Meera burst into the battle-scarred glade, brambles snagging her dress. "Anantnaag!" she cried.

He turned, eyes widening at her disheveled state. Before she could speak, screams rang out as Vishnu's followers surged from the trees. Anantnaag's soldiers scrambled to meet this new threat, the prince spitting curses.

Meera grabbed his arm. "It's a conspiracy! Vishnu means to overthrow you, handing your people to the scientist's devices!" Horror flooded Anantnaag's gaze.

Night fell as rebellion engulfed Naaglok. Despite valiant efforts, Anantnaag's comrades fell back under the tide of betrayal. Doubt clouded the prince's mind - had he lost the faith of all his kin?

As the last village torch flickered out, Anantnaag and Meera fled into the darkness. A heavy silence passed between them before Meera said, "Your people still believe in your heart. We'll rally the loyalists and confront this shadow together."

Anantnaag took a ragged breath. Meera was right - all was not lost if courage still beat in loyal Naaglok breasts. They would face this storm and emerge brighter than before. His people's hope would not die this night. The forest echoed with shouts as rebellion exploded. Anantnaag and Meera fled through the chaos, rallying Naaglok's remaining faithful.

Suddenly, crashes sounded behind them. Whirling, they saw Vishnu's serpent followers giving chase with murderous intent. Anantnaag bared his fangs in a snarl. Meera, run! I'll hold them off!

But as Meera dashed ahead, a large cobra blocked her path with a devious gleam. She screamed and kicked, to no avail as it snatched her, sinking venomous fangs into her shoulder. Meera's world went black.

Anantnaag's eyes blazed furiously at the sight. He let loose a roar that shook the jungle, then met the serpents in a lethal dance. His magic overwhelmed them one by one until only the cobra remained, Meera limp in its coils.

Lay down your life, snake, Anantnaag snarled, her body tearing his resolve to shreds. The cobra laughed cruelly and fled among the trees, taking Meera deeper into danger. Fear for her gripped Anantnaag's heart like a vice - he had failed to protect the one creature brave enough to stand by his side. Now, he knew only one path: pursue their captors to the ends of the earth, and bring Meera home. With a tremendous effort, Anantnaag wrestled his roiling emotions under control. He must think of his people now, not personal vengeance. Landing atop a tall boulder, he called on his magic to amplify his voice across the battlefield.

"Brothers and sisters of Naaglok, hear me! Too long have we let deceitful tongues poison us against each other. I have never desired violence, only peace for our realm. But peace cannot thrive where treachery takes root."

His powerful yet calm tone gave others pause. Some whispered hopefully, others glared in open hatred. But all listened.

"Vishnu has manipulated your anger for his own greed. His dark aims would see us enslaved, not defended. I ask you now - is this truly the fate you want? To become pawns in a mad plot against your king and your kind?"

A few voices called denial, but most wavered in uncertainty. Encouraged, Anantnaag pressed on.

"The ways of deceit and violence will only beget more suffering. I stand before you willing to forgive any wrong, and start anew. Will you turn from shadows and stand with me to rebuild in light?"

His plea hung heavy in the still night air. The people glanced at each other, love and loyalty to their prince slowly rekindling in their eyes. Some came forward, and Anantnaag knew that for now, peace had a chance once more. Anantnaag was losing hope when the jungle seemed to stir around him. A rustle here, birdsong there, guiding his steps. Emerging at a riverbend, he saw the water part as if by invisible hand, revealing footprints in damp sand. A sign from his patron, Lord Shiva.

Renewed, he raced those prints, following their twisting path deeper into Vishnu's territory. At last they led to a dark cave, torches glinting within. Steeling himself, Anantnaag slipped inside to find Meera bound and gagged, Vishnu's minions leering over her limp form.

Vishnu himself spun with a hiss. "So the usurper deigns to join our game. You're too late, brother - Naaglok and this chit's life are mine."

Anantnaag erupted in a furious barrage, fangs and magic swirling. Serpents fell before his onslaught as he fought his way to Meera, breaking her bonds. But numbers told, and Vishnu laughed cruelly even as his followers fell.

With a burst of power that shook the cavern, Anantnaag invoked Shiva's blessing once more, growing to monstrous size. His roar boomed with the might of storms as he lunged for Vishnu. Their battle shook the cave as Meera fled, until at last, the tyrant was defeated. Victory and vengeance were Anantnaag's at last. But the cost of this war had been great for his troubled realm. Anantnaag gently cradled Meera's limp form as they left the collapsing cave. Her eyes fluttered open and she smiled weakly upon seeing him. "The shadow is lifted...for now."

Making camp by a quiet pool, Anantnaag tended Meera's wounds with herbs and magic till dawn's light. As she slept, he looked over his battered yet loyal followers who stood witness.

"Darkness nearly swallowed our light," Anantnaag said. "But together we prevailed against the serpent's venom. Vishnu is defeated - his conspirators scattered to the winds. Yet greater threats loom beyond our borders."

Nagini nodded. "Dr. Ashok and his mysterious masters still intrigue. Their hunger for power remains unchecked."

Anantnaag stroked Meera's hair, finding solace in her steady breaths. "Then our struggles are not ended. I ask only that you stand with me a while longer, as family united against the storm. With courage and compassion guiding our way, Naaglok's hope need never die."

The people roared assent, faith in their rightful king rekindled. Anantnaag smiled, knowing that through loyalty and love, even the darkest of nights would yield to day., There are no more beats outlined for Chapter 4. The chapter ends with unity and resolve restored to Naaglok under Anantnaag's leadership, though greater threats remain. My continuation is:

As Meera's eyes fluttered open, Anantnaag was struck by her indomitable spirit. Though weakened, a flame still burned bright within her. She would make a powerful ally in the battles to come.

For now, recovery was needed. Anantnaag ordered patrols to scout the realm and bring word of any lingering unrest. Naaglok's wounds ran deep, but under the Misty Peaks' watchful gaze, their forests stirred with new life once more.

In the days that followed, Anantnaag ensured supplies and defenses were readied. Though the shadow had retreated, its tendrils still gripped Naaglok in places unseen. With Meera's counsel and Nagini's experience, he was determined to heal both body and soul of his troubled kingdom.

And so ends the tumult of Chapter Four. Through defiance of deceit and the empowering of compassion, unity and peace have been restored to Naaglok under Anantnaag's noble leadership. Yet from the edges of the realm, sinister whispers hint that this is but the lull before a darker storm arises. For now, our heroes rest and recover their strength for the challenges yet to come.

FOUR

Chapter 4: Nature's Wrath

Prince Anantnaag sat pensively in the hollowed ruins of the Ancient Temple, surrounded by his loyal generals. The battle with Vishnu had drained their forces, and still more threats loomed on the horizon.
Nagini approached silently and bowed. "My Lord, scouts report disturbing news. It seems Vishnu's insurrection was but a ploy - he has joined forces with the human Ashok and they march towards Naaglok as we speak."

Anantnaag closed his eyes in dismay. "I had hoped the treachery ended with Vishnu's defeat. It seems the danger has only multiplied." He turned to his generals. "Summon the people. We must prepare to make our stand."

As the order was passed, a familiar figure approached through the rubble - Meera, healed from her ordeals but weariness in her eyes. "The rebels approach from the East," she informed them. "Their numbers are great. But take heart - the forest creatures pledge their support. You shall not face this threat alone."

Anantnaag took her hand gratefully. "Your courage continues to inspire us all. Naaglok is losing this battle - but with unity, we can yet win the war. Sound the horns - it is time we showed our enemies the true power of Nature!"
Anantnaag sprung into action, summoning his generals for urgent orders. The elders will lead our people deeper into the forest sanctuaries, he declared. Nagini, ensure all villagers reach safety.

As the evacuation commenced, Meera approached. Let me stay and fight, she pleaded. My people know these lands - we can set traps and buy you time.

Anantnaag hesitated. It is too dangerous. Vishnu means to wipe us out - I could not bear to see you harmed.

But my place is here, with you, Meera insisted. Your people are now my own. Please, let me stand at your side.

Seeing her resolve, Anantnaag relented. Very well. Work with Nagini to lay ambushes. And Meera - be careful. We have yet more to fight for.

She smiled. As do you, my prince. Now go - lead your armies. We shall hold the line till you return victorious!

With a grateful nod, Anantnaag sped into the forest. The fates of Naaglok and the humans rested on this battle. But with allies like Meera, hope still lived in his heart. The final stand was nigh!, Anantnaag emerged from the foliage with his armies, the last rays of sunlight glinting off their scales. Across the clearing, Vishnu's forces assembled with Dr. Ashok at their lead.

Vishnu slithered forward with a sneer. You are a fool, Anantnaag. Surrender now, and I may spare what is left of your people. Ashok has shown us the power of science - nature will not prevail this day!

Anantnaag curled his hands around his trident. Your lies no longer sway anyone, Vishnu. We defend not just our realm, but the balance all beings depend on. Dr. Ashok sees nature only as a plaything for his experiments - he will not rest until our gifts are ripped from the earth.

From his perch, Ashok laughed harshly. Your magic is meaningless against technology, snake. When I am done, your worthless kingdom will be no more than a footnote in my journals. Surrender - or face annihilation!

Gripping his weapon, Anantnaag called back calmly. We would rather return to the soil than live as your slaves. Naaglok! For nature and freedom - let none stand in our way!

With a mighty roar, the armies surged forth as the skies turned dark. The final battle between science and sorcery was about to begin. The clearing erupted into chaos as the opposing sides slammed together. Anantnaag wielded his trident to devastating effect, blasting rebels into trees with bolts of lightning. But Vishnu fought with equal ferocity, dividing the earth to trap Naaglok armies in fissures.

Elsewhere, Dr. Ashok unleashed his metal war beasts, which spat fire and acid that melted naaglok scales. For each beast felled by magic, two more arose, driving back Anantnaag's troops.

Soon the prince found himself backed against a banyan, flanked by only his most loyal warriors. He flung shards of magic that shattered war machines, but the damage was done. Most of his army lay stunned or beaten across the field.

Just then, an earth-shaking roar turned all eyes skyward. A monstrous shape darkened the skies - a giant cobra, summoned by Vishnu's magic, that lashed its blazing gaze across the clearing.

As it swooped towards the retreating prince, hope seemed lost. But through the tumult arose a clarion battle cry - "For Naaglok!" Meera's village peoples charged like a torrent from the treeline, wielding fallen branches as spears. The tide was set to turn once more. But would it be enough to change their fortunes in the end? Anantnaag grasped his trident tightly, calling on its ancient magics. As the cobra swooped down, he spun the prongs above his head, casting shimmering illusions across the sky.

The cobra shrieked as duplicates of itself filled its vision, confusing it with phantoms. It crashed to the ground in a thrash of scales, stunned. Meanwhile, tree spirits Ans serpents of lightning rose from the earth at Anantnaag's summoning, engaging Vishnu's forces in battle.

Meera fought like a whirlwind, darting between rebels with her spear. She parried blows with grace born of days spent in Naaglok's glades. Seeing her valor, the villagers found new strength, pushing back the invaders with roars.

Dr. Ashok roared in fury and directed his war machines at Meera's group. But Anantnaag intercepted the acid blasts with shields of solid air, protecting his allies. With the trident empowering him, Anantnaag grew to a towering giant, seizing machine after machine in mighty fists.

The tide turned completely as Naaglok magic bonded man and nature against the interlopers. Seeing his forces crumbling, Vishnu called a retreat, glaring daggers at the victorious Anantnaag. The clearing fell silent but for the crackle of burning steel. Against all odds, the enemies of Naaglok had been defeated this day! The fallen machines shimmered and reformed, merging into a towering colossus under Ashok's control. At its helm gazed the pale Entity, eyes blazing with power that dwarfed even Vishnu.

"Fools," it hissed. "Your magic is but noise compared to what I offer." The colossus slammed a fist down, cracking the earth. Anantnaag parried the blow with his trident but was thrown back, crimson trickling from his mouth.

All seemed lost until Meera stepped forth, unafraid. "You fight for greed alone," she declared. "But we battle to protect the bonds between all beings. As long as even one stands with courage against you, your machinations will never succeed!"

Her words ignited something deep within the Naagloks. They surged forth with renewed ferocity, shielding their fallen prince. When Anantnaag regained consciousness, he saw their unity and drew strength from it, channeling the trident's full might into a single, earth-shattering blast.

Cracks tore across the colossus as nature's wrath was unleashed. Meera fought at the vanguard, a beacon of hope. With a last, anguished shriek, the Entity's machine collapsed in a shower of rubble. They had won, but greater trials still lay ahead to secure Naaglok's destiny. Anantnaag and Meera stood amongst the ruins, worn but unbowed. As the Entity rose from the wreckage, a skeletal amalgamation of metal and void, its fury knew no bounds.

"You have not won," it rasped. Shadows coiled around it, swelling its form once more. It lunged towards the pair with malevolent glee.

But Anantnaag and Meera stood ready. When the Entity struck, they evaded together, dancing a lethal waltz around its blows. Anantnaag wielded magical lances of force while Meera spiraled beneath, disrupting its cohesion with targeted strikes.

Bit by bit, the Entity was rent asunder. Yet still it fought on through sheer indomitable will, summoning the remnants of Ashok's army for a final charge.

"Together now, as one!" cried Anantnaag, taking Meera's hand. Their energies fused into a nova that illuminated the darkening woods. With a hellish shriek, the Entity came apart, dispersed on the cosmic winds.

The battlefield fell silent. Meera embraced Anantnaag, tears of relief in her eyes. At long last, the threats to Naaglok had been vanquished. Nature and her guardians were triumphant. A new dawn was breaking over the secret kingdom. With the last of its minions fallen, the Entity turned to face Anantnaag alone. Its tattered form vibrated with malevolent energy, readying some terrible final assault.

Anantnaag interposed himself before Meera protectively. This ends now, demon, he declared. Your shadows will trouble Naaglok no more.

The Entity chuckled oscely. You amuse me, snake, but your games are at an end. With a roar, it swooped towards Anantnaag with shadowy claws outstretched.

Anantnaag met its charge, and the clearning erupted with explosive force as the two titans clashed. Searing attacks rent the earth, lighting the night with an unholy glow. Anantnaag blasted the Entity with blasts of violet lightning, but its form dissolved into smoke, reformed endlessly.

From behind, Meera shouted words of encouragement, bolstering Anantnaag's resolve. With a furious bellow, Anantnaag summoned all the power of Naaglok into his trident, channeling Nature's wrath. At the peak of its arc, reality seemed to rend. A blinding nova exploded outwards.

As the light faded, the Entity lay shattered amongst the ruins, an unearthly wail its dying breath. Anantnaag stood victorious, supported by Meera's arms. At long last, the battle was won. Naaglok was free once more. The ruins fell silent as the Entity's final cries faded. Anantnaag looked out over the destruction, relief mingling with sorrow for those lost.

But amidst the rubble, a chill laughter echoed cruelly. Vishnu emerged from the shadows, scales rent but madness burning in his eyes. "You may have defeated that monster," he hissed, "But Naaglok will never be free so long as I live!"

With a snap of his fangs, Vishnu vanished into the forest once more. Anantnaag knew the serpent would not relinquish his designs so easily. Though the greatest threats were vanquished this day, the war was not yet won.

Meera held Anantnaag's weary frame. "Come, let us leave this place of death. Your people need you whole once more." As they departed into the glades of restoration, Anantnaag vowed that though peace had returned, Vishnu's poison would not be allowed to fester unchecked.

The battle may be over, but the battle for Naaglok's destiny waged on. Only by purging the last roots of hatred could the realm know true freedom again. And so their fight would continue, until every last threat to nature's balance was no more. The people of Naaglok watched their Prince with weary hope as he addressed them amidst the ruins. Though the skies wept for their fallen kin, Anantnaag's words stirred courage in their hearts once more.

"This day we have thwarted those who saw our gifts as sport for domination. But the flames of hatred still linger, and from their ashes new evils may yet rise. We must stand united to douse these flames, and build in their place bonds of trust between all in this land."

Meera stepped forth, taking Anantnaag's hand. "Our vision is one where nature and humanity walk as siblings, not rivals. Together let our hands shape this dream into reality!"

The crowd roared as one, pledging to aid the rebuilding. Anantnaag smiled, turning to greet the Elders emerging from the glades - and his gratefulness grew more profound as the people of the villages followed, bringing gifts of fruit and flowers.

Nature had prevailed this day through the bravery of many. And though dark paths still crossed their forest home, by standing as one, Anantnaag knew Naaglok would thrive forevermore under its kindly watch.

FIVE

Chapter 5: A New Dawn

With the army retreated into the shadows of the forest, Vishnu nursed his wounds both physical and mental. Failure was an alien concept to the serpentine rebel, one who had always known dominance over his kin. Yet now, bested by the supposed weakling Anantnaag and his human allies, the taste of defeat was acrid on his tongue.

From his hiding place within the twisted roots of an ancient banyan, Vishnu spied Dr. Ashok stomping through the undergrowth, cursing Naaglok and its people. A pale gash marred the scientist's cheek where Meera had raked him with her nails during their skirmish. "The whole lot of freaks must be wiped out before they can withstand our machines again," Ashok seethed to his remaining cronies.

Vishnu slipped from his refuge, alert but unseen. Now was the time for new plots to be hatched, revenge to be planned in the shadows while Anantnaag believed the battles won. Naaglok's traitorous prince would know no peace so long as the rebellious serpent drew breath. And this Dr. Ashok, with his scarring grudge against nature's magic, might yet prove a useful tool in tearing down the walls of the kingdom, ripping down all Anantnaag held dear.

Within the tortured recesses of his mind, Vishnu began to weave fresh strands of dissent and deceit. The war was far from over; this was merely the end of the first act. In the healing groves of Naaglok's verdant heart, Meera moved softly amongst the injured, dressing wounds and offering words of comfort. Anantnaag worked beside her, using his magic to draw out toxins and speed the mending of broken flesh. Their eyes met with a sorrowful understanding, yet underneath lay a strength born of unity against the threats that plagued this sacred land.

As she bound bandages about a warrior's torso, Meera spoke quietly. "Naaglok shall have no greater champion than you, Anantnaag. And I vow to stand by your side as you purge this kingdom of those who sow strife and corruption."

Anantnaag took her hand in gratitude. "Your courage and compassion gave us victory today. This is as much your home as the forest you were born in. Let no shadows of the past or promises given in haste divide us now - our fates are entwined, for however long the gods decree."

Outside, the sun's last rays caressed the tapestry of leaves, lighting Meera's smile with a warmth to match the reassurance in Anantnaag's eyes. Through trials yet unknown, their bond would shield Naaglok from the machinations of those who sought its downfall. In each other, prince and human found the strength to face whatever darkness descended upon the realm. Under a dawn still bruised with shadow, Anantnaag called the tribes of Naaglok to a sacred glade untouched by violence. Here, amidst circling pillars long witness to the ebb and flow of history, the prince addressed his people.

Though storms have tested our unity, none have torn asunder the bonds between this land and those who have stewarded her beauty since time immemorial. Rebuilding commences this day, so that future generations may know Naaglok as a realm of refuge, not ruin.

Yet while our walls stand strong once more, subtle thorns still dot the vine that is harmony. Vigilance must remain our virtue until those who sow terror in science's guise, or poison trust with deceit's blade, emerge from the mist to threaten our peace no more.

As one, we have prevailed against powers that would destroy all we hold dear. As one, under your guidance, Anantnaag, we shall outlast whatever new challenges arise. Naaglok is eternal - her children, indomitable. Our foes' defeat was but prelude to the peace our children's children shall know.

To these words, and to Anantnaag's proven leadership, the tribes pledged unity. Work and watch began amidst songs of hope, though shadows lingered at the forest's edge, and fragile was the bud of newborn calm. But together, Naaglok would thrive., Deep in the primal heart of the forest, Meera sang to the birds amidst the ancient trees. Though repairs progressed throughout Naaglok, she felt drawn to lend her voice to this glade where new growth spiraled ever upwards.

Yet as her melody reached its crescendo, a poisoned dart pierced her shoulder. Meera stumbled, vision swimming, only to be seized in ropes of writhing green. From the shadows slipped Vishnu, eyes dancing with malice.

"Sweet music with a fatal note, little morsel," he crooned. "Your prince will come, never fear - for the trap is set."

True to Vishnu's whispers, word reached Anantnaag of Meera's capture, carried on the breath of birds mobilized to serve their mistress. Wasting no time, he traced her aura to a glen darkened by deceit. Within, Dr. Ashok attended to crude machinations, and Meera lay bound, poison stealing her strength.

Anantnaag emerged, eyes aglow with magic and wrath in equal measure. "Release her, and face your demise like the coward you are, Vishnu!" But shadows teemed, and a net of foul sciences was poised to ensnare the unwary. Now, Meera's life hung in the balance of a duel among monsters and magic, where the thinnest thread could mean salvation - or destruction for Naaglok eternally. Vishnu gloated as the trap closed around Anantnaag. With Meera's life held hostage and monsters of steel and sorcery at his command, even Naaglok's prince was finally outmatched.

But Anantnaag stood defiant, magic swirling in preparation to shield Meera from all harm, whatever the cost. His eyes found hers, shining with the strength of bonds forged beyond betrayal or force of arms. Have faith, my brave Champion of the Glades, he urged silently. All will be well.

As Vishnu railed and Ashok sneered, Meera felt newfound purpose awaken within. This land, these people, had become her own - she would not submit tamely while evil had its way. Mustering her failing strength, Meera called out in the tongues of leaf and scale.

All around, the forest roared in answer. Vines and branches ensnared the machines, serpents of lightning whipped from the trees in Anantnaag's defense. As Vishnu howled in fury, Meera flung aside her bonds and grasped the fallen dagger, freeing Anantnaag from his foes' closing grip.

Together, Naaglok's champions stood ready to reclaim the future, whatever allies fate saw fit to send to their side. Victory would be theirs, through compassion's power more than any magic under the sun., With the last foul machine crumbling into ruin, Vishnu saw at last that his schemes were defeated. Dr. Ashok lay stunned amidst fallen gears and wiring, his mad dreams shattered. Only the rebel serpent remained, poisonous to the last.

"Surrender, and you shall be judged justly," called Anantnaag. But Vishnu slithered into the shadow of the trees, vowing to haunt Naaglok from the fringes of the earth. His treason was ended, though traces may linger.

Anantnaag turned to Meera, weary but triumphant. "By your heart and the forest's blessings are we made whole once more. Naaglok owes you a debt beyond repayment, my brave Champion."

Meera smiled. "Your people are my own. Let us rebuild in peace, as friends to all who wish it."

Above, the golden sun broke through frayed clouds. Its warmth soaked into weary souls, casting the healing balm of assured tomorrows upon a land finally free. Hand in hand, Anantnaag and Meera left that place, hope rekindled in their eyes along with passion that would stand the test of time. In the glades they cherished, the future awaited. Deep in the heart of the forest glade, where greenery wove its tapestry around them once more, Anantnaag turned to Meera, taking her hands in his own. His eyes, aglow with magic and affection, sought permission to illuminate the path ahead.

"My brave Champion," he said, "your love has banished shadows from this realm. Will you remain at my side as Naaglok's beacon of hope and unity? I offer you a place in these groves, and in my heart, for all our days."

Meera's smile was radiant as sunrise. "There is no home I cherish more. I will stand with your people as their voice beyond these borders, so that never again may division arise. And I offer you my love, now and always, my beloved prince."

Their kiss sealed a bond infinite as the forest. Hand in hand, Naaglok's monarchs walked side by side to share their joy with those they pledged to guide. Though perils may lurk still in life's wild groves, compassion triumphed through their union. And where Anantnaag and Meera stood, a new dawn of understanding was sure to bloom. Many seasons passed in peace across the realm of Naaglok, as Anantnaag and Meera's loving guidance nurtured growth of both forest and fellowship. Though Vishnu's toxic whispers could still be sensed at twilight, none dared breach the unity defended by king and queen.

In glades once stalked by fear, children of scale and leaf learned and played without concern. Beyond Naaglok's boughs, too, hearts once closed to mysteries beyond understanding had blossomed open, finding friendship where once was writ only distrust.

Change came, as it must - but it was change emboldened by compassion. Anantnaag smiled to see villages dot forest clearings where ash once fell, humans and naaglok mingling in marketplaces alive with song. And deeper still amid green bowers, magic remained: in mysteries wizened tribes kept, and in eyes where starry constellations seemed to swirl.

Here, with legacy secured and realm thriving in balance, the tale of Naaglok ends - yet its triumph echoes on. For where love stands sentinel, and understanding lights the way, even shadows bleakest cannot quench hope's flame. Such is the eternal lesson of this hidden land: that by embracing all children of this earth, we become more than conquerors of Strife. We become family. Thus ends the tale of Naaglok - for now. May its lessons uplift all who journeyed here: that through unity, courage of heart, and resolute defense of lands and bonds we cherish, even the darkest of tempests may be weathered. Science and magic learned to live not as opposites but complements; nature's mysteries remained secure yet shared.

Most of all, may Naaglok's triumph inspire each soul to see past surface into heart: to forge alliances where once were boundaries, and greet the unfamiliar with empathy instead of fear. Its champions Anantnaag and Meera proved such understanding conquerors of Strife - as will any who embrace this story's gifts of hope.

Adventure called our heroes to new horizons after peace was won. But Naaglok's magic lives on wherever friendship bridges seeming divides, and communities choose compassion over division. Its legacy will thrive as long as such seeds take root in minds and hearts open to growth.

Let this tale spread therefore on whispers through the wildwood, a beacon to light pathways and nourish dreams. Naaglok faces no ending - merely new genesis, as certainty gives way to possibility anew. May the fruits of its love for all seasons bless their guardians, and this first act prove but first page in an odyssey yet unfolding. Farewell, for now, and fair winds!

www.ingramcontent.com/pod-product-compliance
Lightning Source LLC
LaVergne TN
LVHW070944160826
845679LV00022B/1908

* 9 7 9 8 8 9 2 7 7 4 6 3 5 *